Mark Twain (1835-1910) was the pseudonym of the American novelist Samuel Langhorne Clemens, who was born in Florida, Missouri. *The adventures of Tom Sawyer* was first published in 1876, and was followed in 1884 by *The adventures of Huckleberry Finn.*

© Creation, script and illustrations: A. M. Lefèvre, M. Loiseaux, M. Nathan-Deiller, A. Van Gool.
First published and produced by **Creations for Children International,** Belgium. www.c4ci.com
This edition published by BPI INDIA PVT LTD
16, Ansari Road, Darya Ganj, New Delhi-110002
Tel: +91-11-2328 4898, 2327 6118 Fax: +91-11-23271653
Email: bpiindia@airtelmail.in • info@bpiindia.com

Tom Sawyer

illustrated by
'''VAN GOOL'''

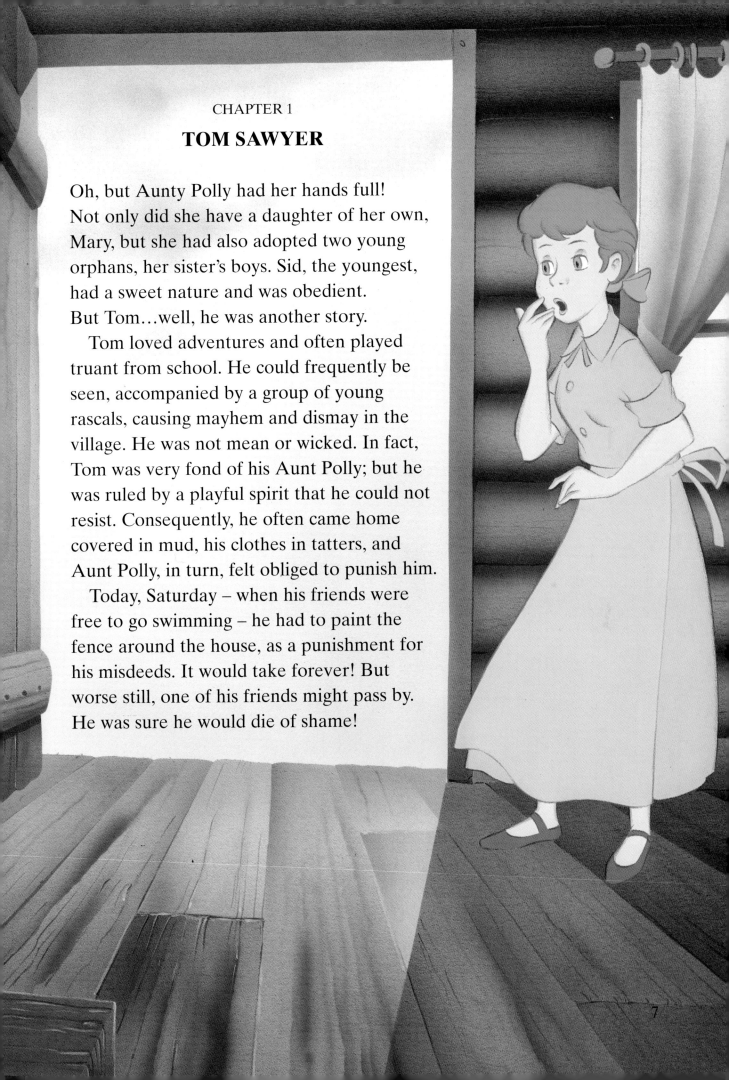

CHAPTER 1

TOM SAWYER

Oh, but Aunty Polly had her hands full!
Not only did she have a daughter of her own,
Mary, but she had also adopted two young
orphans, her sister's boys. Sid, the youngest,
had a sweet nature and was obedient.
But Tom…well, he was another story.

Tom loved adventures and often played
truant from school. He could frequently be
seen, accompanied by a group of young
rascals, causing mayhem and dismay in the
village. He was not mean or wicked. In fact,
Tom was very fond of his Aunt Polly; but he
was ruled by a playful spirit that he could not
resist. Consequently, he often came home
covered in mud, his clothes in tatters, and
Aunt Polly, in turn, felt obliged to punish him.

Today, Saturday – when his friends were
free to go swimming – he had to paint the
fence around the house, as a punishment for
his misdeeds. It would take forever! But
worse still, one of his friends might pass by.
He was sure he would die of shame!

Oh! Horror of horrors! Ben Rogers was ambling around the corner. What was Tom to do?

"Remain calm and dignified," he told himself, "act nonchalantly...." Tom decided to adopt the pose of an artist at work. Ben Rogers was impressed, particularly as Tom seemed to be enjoying himself.

"I say Tom, could I help?" he asked.

Tom hesitated. After all, painting Aunt Polly's fence required skill and concentration. After much deliberation, he agreed. Soon Ben was hard at work, and as each of Tom's friends passed by they, too, begged to be allowed to paint the fence. Tom, happily, distributed paintbrushes, then went to doze in the shade of a tree. Aunt Polly could hardly believe her eyes when, a few hours later, she came to inspect Tom's progress. The job was finished and the fence had received not one, but two coats of paint!

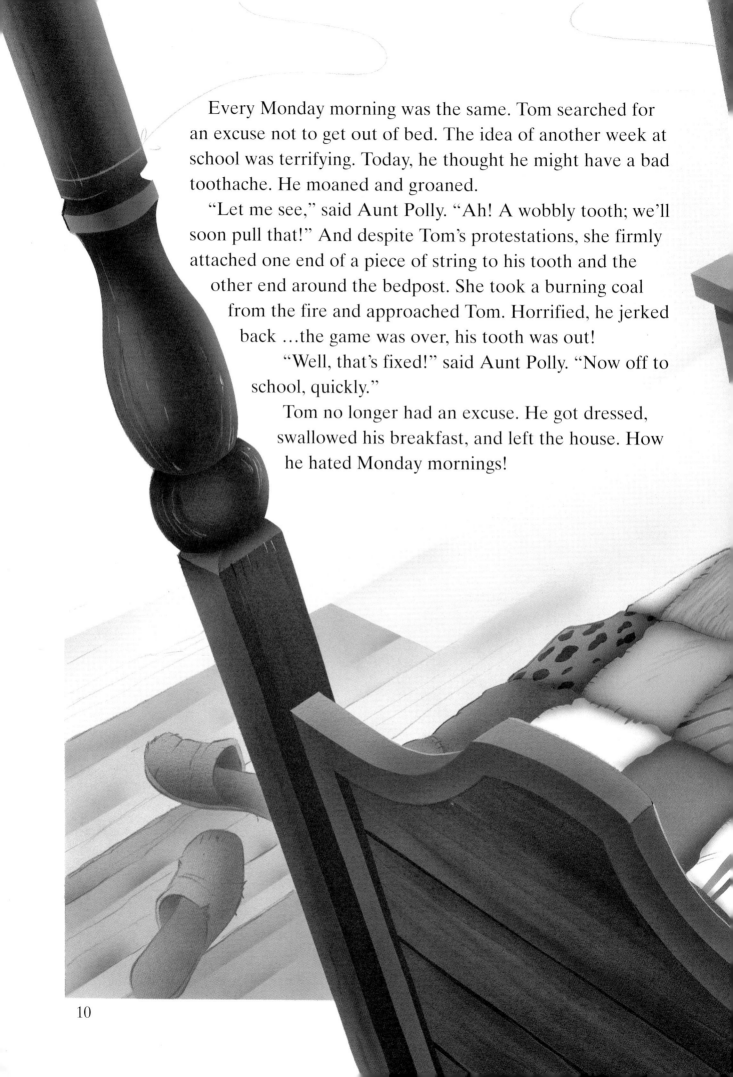

Every Monday morning was the same. Tom searched for an excuse not to get out of bed. The idea of another week at school was terrifying. Today, he thought he might have a bad toothache. He moaned and groaned.

"Let me see," said Aunt Polly. "Ah! A wobbly tooth; we'll soon pull that!" And despite Tom's protestations, she firmly attached one end of a piece of string to his tooth and the other end around the bedpost. She took a burning coal from the fire and approached Tom. Horrified, he jerked back …the game was over, his tooth was out!

"Well, that's fixed!" said Aunt Polly. "Now off to school, quickly."

Tom no longer had an excuse. He got dressed, swallowed his breakfast, and left the house. How he hated Monday mornings!

But he soon changed his mind. "Well! Well! There might be something to be gained by going to school," he thought when he met the new pupil in his class.

Her name was Becky Thatcher. She was the new judge's daughter. Her hair was wispy and blond, and she had the eyes of a princess and the smile of an angel! Tom immediately fell in love, and while the teacher's back was turned he passed her a tiny package. Inside he had enclosed a small ring and on the paper he had written: *Becky, I luv you*

Becky didn't even look up, but she put the trinket in her pocket.

"Well, that's a start," thought Tom, and he spent the rest of the day with his head in the clouds.

CHAPTER 2

MURDER IN THE CEMETERY

That evening, in bed, Tom was thinking of Becky and nearly forgot about his rendezvous with Huck, his best friend. Huckleberry Finn's mother was dead, and his father, a good-for-nothing, had abandoned Huck long ago. Tom considered Huck to be extremely fortunate – he lived in a barrel with no one to make him wash or go to school.

Tom had agreed to meet Huck at midnight in the cemetery. They were going to test a new spell. So, quickly and quietly, he got dressed and slipped out of the bedroom window. It didn't take long to reach the cemetery, where he spotted his friend crouched behind a gravestone. Huck signaled Tom to crawl down beside him without saying a word; someone else was already in the graveyard. Tom listened carefully. He could hear Indian Joe's voice: "Hand over the money or I'll kill you!"

He was talking to Doc Robinson!

"Never," replied the doctor, firmly.

Suddenly, the boys heard a third voice. It was Muff Potter, a good sort when he was sober. But tonight, like most nights, he was drunk.

"Ca…ca…calm down, gentlemen!" he stammered. But before he knew what had happened, and in the confusion, Potter had been hit over the head by the doctor. He collapsed, close to the boys!

Tom and Huck, petrified, shrank back into the shadows. They could see Indian Joe brandishing a knife, its sharp blade shining in the moonlight.

"The money or your life!" growled Indian Joe.

Not willing to accede, the doctor raised his stick; but the Indian was too quick for him. He plunged his knife into the doctor's chest. The doctor crumpled and fell to the ground. He was dead!

Indian Joe remained calm. He rifled the doctor's pockets and stole his money. Then he turned toward Muff, who was still lying senseless on the ground. Indian Joe slipped the knife into Muff's hand before he left the cemetery.

"What are we going to do?" Tom asked, shaking.

"For the moment, nothing," replied Huck. "You must not tell a soul! We'll see what happens tomorrow."

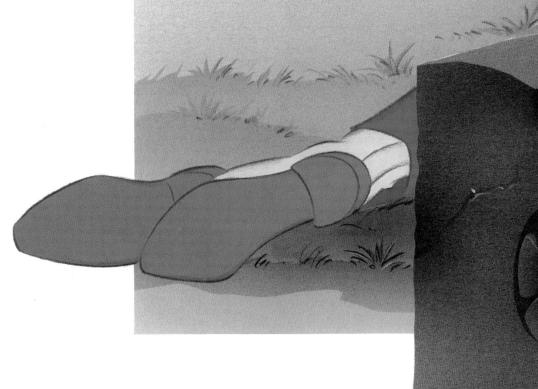

The following day, for the first time, Tom was happy to go to school. He had been tossing and turning all night. He'd had nightmares and was counting on pretty Becky to distract him. Alas, another blow awaited him: the ring was on his desk. It had been returned with a short note:

Mr. Sawyer
You must learn to spell before writing
to young ladies. Also, my hair is blond,
and I understand that you prefer redheads…
Becky Thatcher

Tom immediately understood. In front of him the redheaded Amy Lawrence was smirking. What a nuisance! She must have told Becky that she used to be Tom's girlfriend…. Before Tom could sort out this misunderstanding, the teacher burst into the room.

"A horrible murder took place in the cemetery last night," he announced. "There will be no school today."

Twenty minutes later, Tom met Huck in the cemetery. Everyone from the village was there, standing in a group around Doctor Robinson's body. Muff Potter had also been discovered, asleep, at the scene of the crime.

"Look! His knife is covered in blood," said Indian Joe. He was standing calmly in the middle of the crowd! Tom and Huck couldn't believe their eyes. If they denounced him now, Indian Joe would, no doubt, defend himself with a plausible story. No one would believe their account of the previous evening's events. Anyway, if Tom and Huck were to speak out, Indian Joe would certainly wreak a terrible revenge. What, after all, were another couple of bodies to a murderer?

Afraid, the boys decided to keep quiet. But they were sick with shame when Muff Potter was arrested for the murder. The poor man didn't even try to defend himself. He had no recollection of the previous night's events, and he knew that he had been found next to the body, his knife – covered in blood – in his hand. He also had a horrendous hangover! Without protest, Muff was led away to the local jail.

CHAPTER 3
THE PIRATES' OATH

Tom's terrible nightmares continued. He dreamt that Muff Potter had been hanged, and Indian Joe was spreading terror throughout the village! One night, Tom cried out in his sleep:

"Help! Help! Please don't kill me…"

"What's the matter?" groaned Sid, waking up with a fright.

"What? Me? Nothing at all. You must be dreaming," replied Tom. But Sid wasn't fooled, and the following day he spoke to Aunt Polly.

"That child worries me," she sighed. And to calm Tom's nerves she stood him in the garden and poured several buckets of cold water over his head. But it was Tom's conscience, not his nerves, that needed soothing. He often visited Muff Potter in prison, taking him an apple or a piece of cake.

"At least," repeated Muff, "you are a decent young man." Tom felt doubly guilty.

If only he had a smile from Becky to console him. But she didn't miss an opportunity to mock Tom. There was only one solution: he must run away!

Tom had no problem convincing Huck and Joe Harper, another of his close friends, to join his adventure. As pirates, they would board a raft and sail down the Mississippi to a hideaway on Jackson Island.

"We are going to be the most desperate pirates on the river!" declared Tom.

So one morning, instead of going to school, the friends set off down the river. In his satchel, instead of schoolbooks, Tom had packed provisions: bread, apples, and a whole ham!

"Well done!" said Huck. "I've brought our survival equipment: a line and bait for fishing, three spears for hunting, and three knives for protection. Pirates should have cutlasses, but these knives will do!"

As for Joe Harper, he brought a large burning coal so that they could start a campfire.

After a smooth crossing, the pirates landed on the island. They went swimming, had a sumptuous banquet of bread and ham, and then explored their new domain. The island was completely deserted, so they staked their claim – it now belonged to the desperados!

"We must swear allegiance to each other, and agree never to return to the village," proposed Tom. So, hand on hand, they took a solemn oath.

But as evening fell, each boy began to long for home. Suddenly, they heard the noise of an engine.

The ferryboat was towing a number of smaller boats carrying men with lanterns.

"They're looking for us!" whispered Tom. Tom, Huck, and Joe felt like heroes. If they were not discovered, they would become legends in their own time. So they quickly agreed to hide deep in the woods.

Three days and three nights passed. Convinced the boys had drowned, the men of the village abandoned their search. The pastor rang the church bells solemnly. All the villagers, dressed in mourning, flocked to hear him preach.

"A great tragedy has hit our community," announced the pastor from his pulpit. "Three admirable young boys have perished, and they will be sorely missed by us all."

Hunched together in one of the front pews, Aunt Polly, Mary, and Sid were quietly crying. Three rows behind them, a young girl sitting between her mother and father was sobbing loudly: it was Becky Thatcher! No vision could have been sweeter to Tom's eyes. For Tom was there, in church, as were Huck and Joe! The three of them were attending their own funeral!

The boys had heard the church bells ringing. Their adventure over, they were on their way home when they discovered a service was being held for them. Unable to resist the temptation to attend unobserved, Tom, Huck, and Joe hid behind the church door and listened to the flattering eulogies.

"Be consoled, my brothers and sisters," cried the pastor. "We'll meet them again in Heaven."

"Now!" said Tom, and the three boys dashed down the main aisle, to the great amazement of the congregation. Joe Harper's mother fainted. And as for Aunt Polly, she hurled herself at Tom and hugged him tightly to make sure she was not dreaming. She was so happy that she forgot to punish him. But Tom's greatest surprise came when Becky kissed him!

For days afterwards Tom recounted, in detail and with much embellishment, the events of the three days and three heroic nights, spent under the stars, on Jackson Island.

CHAPTER 4

THE TREASURE HUNT

"The great disadvantage of being a hero, and trying to remain one, is that you have to behave like one all the time," Tom reflected three days later, when he attended Muff Potter's trial.

The whole village turned up in court. They had already made up their minds that Muff Potter was guilty! Five character witnesses were called. Muff was bad, he was a drunkard! Without a doubt, he would be hanged. Indian Joe, in particular, was most adamant about the verdict!

Hesitantly, Tom stood up and asked to testify. He was shaking all over, for he dreaded the Indian's knife between his shoulder blades. But he was firmly resolved to tell the truth. He took an oath on the Bible, and then told the judge what he had seen on the night of the crime. Everyone in the courtroom was amazed by the new evidence, and confusion reigned for several minutes. Indian Joe took advantage of the commotion to quickly slip away.

Tom's nightmares returned. Undoubtedly, he was a hero. But he trembled at the very thought of Indian Joe's revenge.

Happily, Huck was there to distract him. One day Tom visited Huck at home, in his barrel, and found him greatly excited.

"Yesterday, when I was passing the haunted house," said Huck, "I saw two suspicious fellows go in. A tall, thin man and the deaf-mute Spaniard who has been hanging around the village for the past few days. They looked like conspirators. I said to myself, 'I'll return with Tom to investigate.' Let's go now."

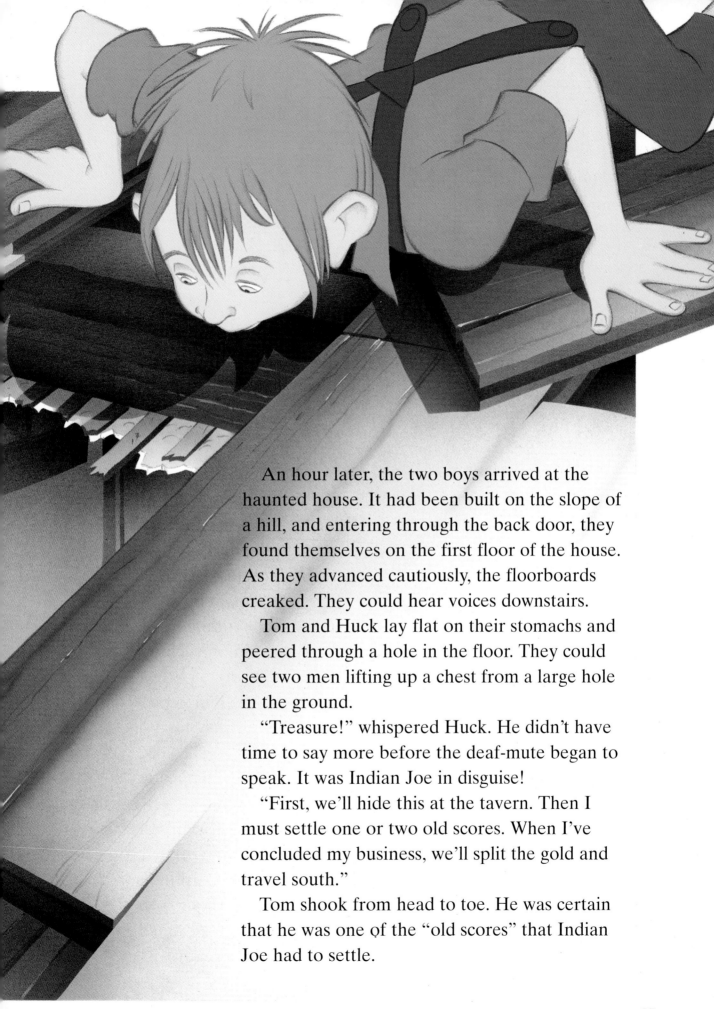

An hour later, the two boys arrived at the haunted house. It had been built on the slope of a hill, and entering through the back door, they found themselves on the first floor of the house. As they advanced cautiously, the floorboards creaked. They could hear voices downstairs.

Tom and Huck lay flat on their stomachs and peered through a hole in the floor. They could see two men lifting up a chest from a large hole in the ground.

"Treasure!" whispered Huck. He didn't have time to say more before the deaf-mute began to speak. It was Indian Joe in disguise!

"First, we'll hide this at the tavern. Then I must settle one or two old scores. When I've concluded my business, we'll split the gold and travel south."

Tom shook from head to toe. He was certain that he was one of the "old scores" that Indian Joe had to settle.

Huck and Tom agreed to watch the tavern and follow the bandits to see where they stashed the treasure. But the following day, instead of joining Huck, Tom was distracted by an invitation from Becky. Mr. and Mrs. Thatcher had arranged a grand picnic, down river, for all the children of the village. Tom couldn't refuse, particularly as no adults were allowed on the trip. So he decided to forget his troubles and enjoy himself.

Becky stayed by his side on the voyage downstream, and when they landed at the creek she agreed to abandon the others and visit a nearby cave with Tom.

Night had fallen when Huck, still on watch, finally saw the two bandits leave the tavern. They were carrying something heavy. It must be the treasure! Huck decided to follow at a discreet distance, though he could still hear them talking.

"Are you really going to visit the old judge's widow?" inquired the tall man.

"Certainly," replied Indian Joe. "Her husband couldn't wait for my revenge, but I haven't forgotten the long days spent in prison because of his sentence. His wife will have to pay the penalty in his place!"

"It's not Tom, after all, that he's seeking," thought Huck, "but the judge's widow, Mrs. Douglas. What shall I do? I'll have to run back and alert the village. They must save the widow! But…it'll mean that I'll lose track of the treasure! If only Tom were here instead of amusing himself at a ridiculous picnic!" Huck tussled with his conscience. Finally, he abandoned the treasure and turned back. The first house he reached was that of the Welshman. He hammered on the door. Two minutes later, the Welshman and his sons, armed with rifles, were on their way to protect Mrs. Douglas.

41

Heavily laden, the bandits could only travel slowly. Huck and the three men arrived in time to see Indian Joe and the tall man entering Mrs. Douglas' house.

"There they are!" whispered the Welshman. But as they rushed toward the steps of the porch, one of his sons stumbled over a rocking chair. His gun was loaded, and when he fell it fired! Alerted to their presence, the bandits fled into the woods. It was useless following them: it was dark and it would be difficult to find the villains in the dense undergrowth.

When the widow discovered that she'd had a narrow escape from danger, she fell on the Welshman and his sons with grateful thanks.

"It is not us, but Huck whom you must thank," said the Welshman. "He has saved your life."

But Huck was not listening. He had discovered the heavy chest, abandoned by the bandits when they took flight. It wasn't the old chest of the previous day, as he had thought – it was only a trunk full of tools. The treasure must be somewhere else!

CHAPTER 5

THE LABYRINTH

Huck was too tired to return to the tavern to look for the treasure chest. Anyway, he was hungry and Mrs. Douglas had offered him a fine supper. Once he had eaten, she insisted that he stay the night.

"Rest, my child," she said. "You must be exhausted after this evening's chase. Besides, I will feel much safer with a man in the house!"

Huck was unable to refuse her invitation. He didn't enjoy sleeping between sheets. But, just this once, he would make an effort.

Meanwhile, back in the village, the Welshman and his sons found the streets full of people, despite the late hour. It was some minutes before they discovered that Becky Thatcher and Tom Sawyer were missing. They had not returned with the others from the picnic. No one had noticed their absence until the ferryboat had docked!

At first, Tom and Becky had enjoyed their adventure. By candlelight they explored the cave. Wandering down various avenues, they admired the magnificent stalactites and stalagmites. Soon they came upon a deep lake. They skirted the water and ran through a maze of passageways.

Suddenly, in the distance they heard a shrill whistle. It was a signal from the ferryboat. The picnic was over and it was time to return home. They'd better hurry back or the boat would leave without them. They ran in all directions but could not find the way out.

Several hours passed. Soon they were stranded in the dark, for their candles had burnt out. There was no sign of a search party. Becky was tired and hungry. Tom was cross with himself; they should not have wandered so far. It was entirely his fault, and now Becky was frightened. Suddenly, they heard heavy footsteps, and soon a glimmer of light appeared. Becky, relieved, was going to call for help when Tom, terrified, slapped his hand over her mouth. This was no rescue party! The approaching man was none other than Indian Joe!

The men from the village arranged a search party that night. Some scoured the picnic area and the cave, others – in boats – searched the river, but they could not find the children. By lunchtime the following day, the men decided to return home.

Only one small boat remained. It had drifted some way down the creek and was skirting a high cliff when one of the men aboard cried, "Look! Up there!"

He had spotted two silhouettes, high up on the cliff, in a crevice. Tom and Becky were waving furiously to attract his attention.

Tom and Becky were soon home. They were exhausted, hungry, and cold, and they were both suffering from a fever; so no one pressed them for details of their ordeal. After many days, as they slowly recovered, they were able to tell their story.

Tom recalled that, in the cave, Indian Joe had passed close by without seeing them. Later on Tom remembered the ball of kite string in his pocket, and he'd had an idea. He tied one end of the string to a stalagmite and then, as he explored for a way out, he unwound the string. Eventually he entered a gallery in which there was a small opening to the sky. Daylight at last! Tom and Becky struggled through the opening and found themselves on a narrow ledge, high up a cliff. But they were too exhausted to go any farther. As Tom got to this juncture in his story, Judge Thatcher came in: "No one will ever get lost in the labyrinth of that cave again," he announced. "The day of your return, I had the entrance sealed with a heavy oak door that is firmly padlocked and bolted."

"But then," cried Tom, "Indian Joe must still be inside!"

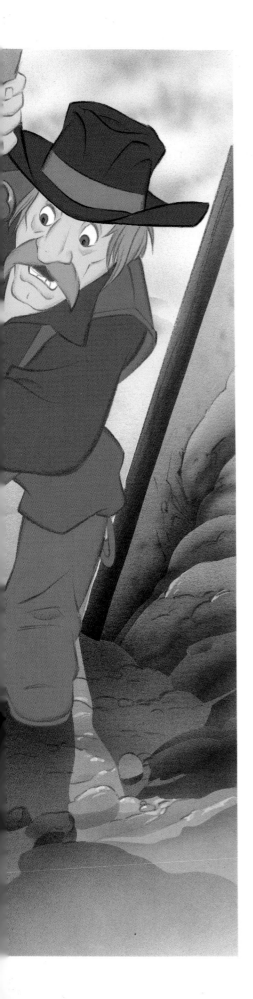

When the villagers returned to the cave, they found not only Indian Joe, but also his accomplice – the tall, thin man. Both were stretched out, dead, behind the door!

On the ground, close by, were their knives, the blades blunt and broken. They had evidently tried to chip their way through the door. Both Indian Joe and his friend had died of hunger and exhaustion. Tom could only imagine their suffering and, although he knew that they were both hardened criminals, he could not help feeling sorry for them.

CHAPTER 6

RICH AT LAST

While Tom was recuperating, Huck came to see him every day. But Aunt Polly eyed him suspiciously. He was, in part, responsible for Tom's waywardness, and so she barred Huck's entry to the sickroom.

However, once Tom was fully recovered he went to see his friend.

"You're looking well," said Huck. "Now we can resume our quest."

"What do you mean?" asked Tom.

"You haven't forgotten the treasure, have you?" exclaimed Huck. "I know it's not at the haunted house or the tavern. I've been to look. Therefore…"

"It's in the cave!" shouted Tom, excitedly.

So the next day, the two adventurers returned to the cave, which they entered, from the riverside, through the small opening in the cliff.

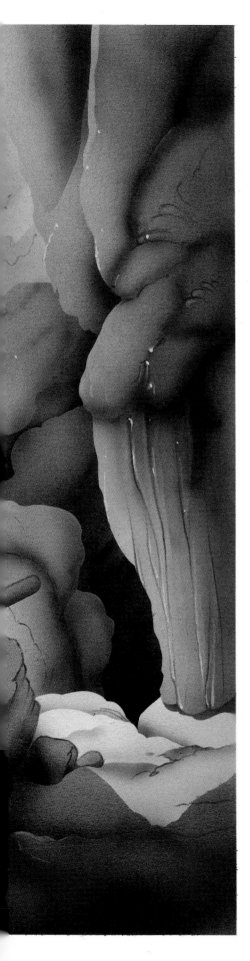

Tom and Huck carried a stock of candles, several large sacks in which to put their booty, and a large ball of string.

Tom bristled with pride as he showed his friend around the cave. After an hour or two they found a recess in one of the cave walls. There was evidence that it had been inhabited. A straw mattress lay on the floor, and there were even several blankets. Without a doubt, this had been the bandits' hiding place. But there was no sign of the treasure chest.

"Look," said Tom. In the soft earth there were footprints that led to a large boulder. Tom and Huck heaved the boulder to one side and there, in an opening in the cave wall, was the chest! They dragged it out and lifted the lid. It was full of gold coins!

"We're rich, we're rich!" the boys cried, dancing around the cave. They could hardly believe their eyes. Soon their sacks were full. They returned to the boat and rowed home. Ashore, laden down like donkeys, they were passing the Widow Douglas' house when one of the village boys called out: "Where have you two rascals been? We have all been waiting for you!"

A large crowd had assembled at the widow's
house, and when Tom and Huck entered they
were warmly welcomed by one and all – with
the exception of Aunt Polly, who was horrified
to see Tom looking so dirty. But Judge
Thatcher didn't give her time to grumble.

"We are here today," he said, "to give Huck
some good news. Mrs. Douglas is so grateful
that he saved her life, that she has decided to
adopt Huck and will ensure that he receives a
good education."

Huck was crestfallen. Indeed, for a moment,
it looked as if he was going to make a quick
dash to escape. But Tom rushed to his rescue.
He quickly fetched the sacks of gold from the
hall and stammered, "Huck is very grateful,
but…he doesn't need an education … he's …
we're rich!"

Tom tipped the sacks of gold onto the
carpet. The crowd was stunned into silence!

It took some time to convince the two friends that riches couldn't replace a good education. For Huck, many ordeals lay ahead of him. He had to learn to wear shoes, use a handkerchief, and sleep, *every* night, in a bed!

Worst of all, Tom and Huck had to relinquish their fortune. The gold was placed in the bank, and except for regular pocket money, they couldn't touch it until they were eighteen! The boys had to say goodbye – for now – to their dreams of banquets, distant travels, and expensive presents. Goodbye also to the necklace Tom had planned to give Becky.

However, this did not mean an end to their adventures!